Praise for *The Underdog Duckling*

"With gorgeous illustrations and thoughtful, beautiful words, this story of Quinn finding his place in a complicated world is told simply and vividly. A treasure."

— Alice Kuipers,
author of *Polly Diamond and the Magic Book*

"A delightfully written and charmingly illustrated story, *The Underdog Duckling* has the power to fill young readers with concern, curiosity, and a measure of hope. Not only is this a story about truth and a little boy coming to grips with his own feelings about change, it is a story about strength and bravery. Well done, Sally Meadows."

— Glynis M. Belec,
award-winning children's author, freelance writer, and inspirational speaker

"The story of the underdog duckling is a beautiful way to experience the suffering and healing of a heartbroken child. I expect that many other children will find healing through the story of Quinn and his special friend."

— Christie Thomas,
author of *Quinn's Promise Rock* and mother of three

"A beautiful story of what it means to find courage and strength from within. The parallels between the underdog duckling and Quinn's own situation will resonate with anyone who has faced the challenge of feeling lost and alone. By finding meaning from nature and the world around us, Meadows has created an impactful narrative that teaches us that in trying times, we'll emerge stronger than ever. A powerful story for families coping with the uncertainty of illness."

— Kristine Scarrow,
author of *The 11th Hour,* and other young adult novels, and hospital writer-in-residence

"The Underdog D[...]
going through a [...]
weaves the theme of personal growth through overcoming adversity into a tender tale that is sure to resonate with young children. Olha Tkachenko's illustrations beautifully enhance the narrative."

— Wendy Crawford,
retired teacher

"Here's a story of inspiration found in nature. When life takes an unexpected turn for young Quinn, he struggles to face the new challenges that arise. Watching an orphaned duckling bravely make its way gives Quinn both the courage he needs, and a new sense of belonging."

— Gillian Richardson,
award-winning author of *10 Plants That Shook The World* and *10 Routes That Crossed the World*

"Meadows and Tkachenko have teamed up to create a lovely story about an underdog duckling. Sally writes with compelling and heart-warming style, and the illustrations compliment her naturalist flavour. A delightful read!"

— Marion Mutala,
national bestselling, award-winning author of the Baba's Babushka tetralogy

"A beautiful reminder to children that it's okay to be sad and scared, and that even when things are tough, there will be light at the end."

— Darla Read,
postpartum doula and parent

THE UNDERDOG
DUCKLING

written by
SALLY MEADOWS

illustrated by
OLHA TKACHENKO

Acknowledgments

I am grateful to live in a city with neighbourhood ponds as wonderfully full of life as the naturally occurring sloughs on the surrounding prairies. Spending time at one such pond only a few blocks from my home always stirs my imagination and gives me the peace that comes only from being in and connected to nature. This story is the fruit of observing the beauty, joy, and drama of the everyday lives of water birds as they unfolded before my very eyes.

Many thanks to authors Sharon Plumb, Alison Lohans, Glynis M. Belec, Miriam Körner, Ashleigh Mattern, and Katherine Lawrence for editing and/or providing feedback at various stages during the writing process. Thanks are also due to my fellow authors, educators, and parents, who kindly provided encouraging words and the lovely reviews found at the beginning of this book.

Olha Tkachenko, you are a beautiful artist: thank you for bringing this story to life with such vivid visuals. To my publisher Heather Nickel, you are the epitome of professionalism and grace; thank you once again for leading me through the publishing process.

This book would not have been possible without the support of my husband and the blessing of my heavenly Father, who gives me such good gifts each and every day.

THE UNDERDOG DUCKLING
story © Sally Meadows, 2018
illustrations © Olha Tkachenko, 2018

Cataloguing data available from Library and Archives Canada.

ISBN: 978-1-988783-30-7

Cover and book design by Heather Nickel.
Printed in Canada.
August 2018

YOUR NICKEL'S WORTH PUBLISHING
Regina, SK.
www.ynwp.ca

Never stop being **you.**

Quinn's eyes blinked open. *Where am I?*

As he reached out to touch the dusty sunbeam, it all came rushing back.

This was Papa's house in the city. Mom was in the hospital.

Quinn swung his legs over the edge of the bed and shuffled into the kitchen.

"Good morning," said Papa as he poured cereal into a bowl. "Ready to check out the new school?"

Butterflies swirled in Quinn's stomach.

He pulled on his favourite rain boots for the walk to school.

When they reached the school entrance, Quinn stopped.

Papa patted his shoulder.

"It'll be fine, Quinn. I'll be right here when you're done."

After school, Papa took Quinn the long way home so they could watch the mallard ducks. When Papa put his arm around Quinn, it was hard not to cry.

And not just about his mom.

Quinn couldn't wait until school ended for the summer.

When the last bell rang on the last day of school, Quinn rushed out. "Can I go home and stay with Dad now?"

"I'm sorry, Quinn," said Papa. "Your dad can't run the farm and take care of you too. You'll stay with me until your mom gets better."

Quinn stomped to the pond's pebbly beach. He picked up two whole fistfuls of rocks and threw them into the water.

Papa took Quinn to the pond every day. He sat and watched while Quinn explored. For a while, Quinn almost forgot his troubles.

One morning, Quinn saw a duckling all by itself. Every time it swam near the other ducks, they chased it away.

Quinn's face got hot. His eyes burned.

Why didn't the other ducks like the duckling?

And why weren't its parents taking care of it?

"What's wrong, son?" asked Papa.

Quinn paced back and forth. He told Papa about the duckling with no friends.

Papa nodded and rubbed his whiskers.

Quinn looked for the duckling every day. The other ducks still pushed it away. But it found its own food, and Quinn could see it was getting bigger.

One morning, Quinn spotted a lady in a red canoe shooing a duckling towards shore with her paddle.

Quinn grabbed Papa's hand. "That's MY duckling! What's she doing?"

The duckling waddled onto shore.

A man swooshed a net over it and put it in a cage. He loaded it in his truck and drove away.

"No!" Quinn ran.

Papa grabbed his arm before he darted onto the road.

All Quinn could think about was *What's going to happen to my duckling?*

Nothing Papa said or did made Quinn feel better. "I think it's time to go see your mom, Quinn."

At the hospital, Quinn climbed onto Mom's bed and snuggled close. He told her about the duckling, trying not to cry.

Then, everything spilled out:

"The kids were mean to me at school. They said my boots smelled like cow poop! No one wanted to be my friend. And I'm scared because you're sick! Why can't things be the way they used to be?"

Mom hugged Quinn. "It's okay to feel sad or angry or scared when it feels like everything is against us, Quinn. That's called being an underdog. Some people think underdogs are weak. But I say they can be strong."

Quinn looked up. He saw the dark under his mom's eyes. He saw the tufts of hair peeking out from her cap. He sat up tall and touched her face.

She kissed his hand and smiled.

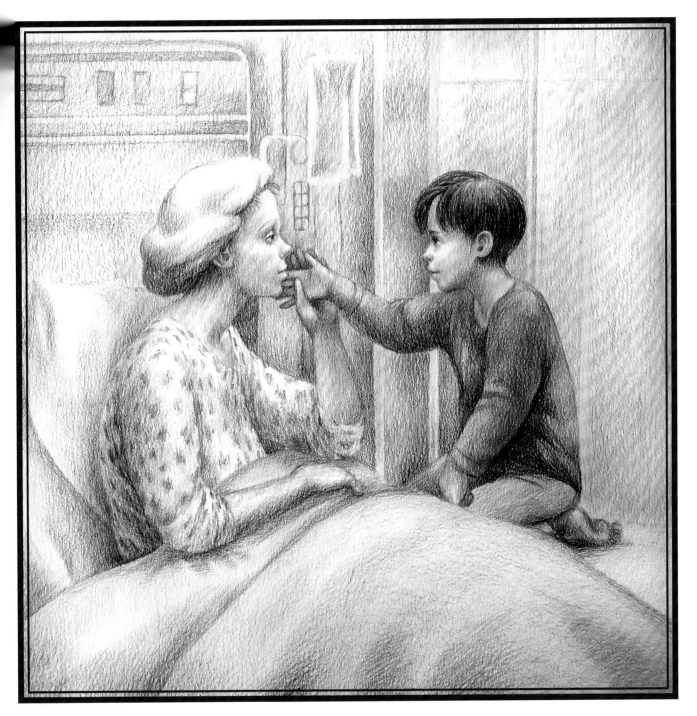

Later, Quinn asked Papa if they could try to find out what happened to the duckling. Papa typed into his computer and wrote down a number. "This man might be able to help us."

Papa put the phone on speaker. Quinn dialed the number.

"Do you know what happened to the duckling at the pond near my Papa's house?" he asked.

"Ah, yes," the man said, after Papa gave the location. "It was an orphaned duckling. We brought it to a safe place outside the city."

It turned out the duckling wasn't a mallard after all. It was an American wigeon. The man explained that wigeon and mallard ducklings look a lot alike.

"So my duckling's going to be okay?" asked Quinn.

"Yes, I believe it will," said the man.

As he tucked Quinn into bed that night, Papa said, "I'm proud of you, Quinn. You are a kind, brave boy. Never stop being you."

Quinn snuggled under the covers. "The duckling was brave too—right, Papa?"

"He sure was, son. He sure was."

When school started again in the fall, Quinn felt butterflies in his stomach.

But when Papa came to pick him up, Quinn couldn't help smiling.

He had a new friend, Sam.

As the days got shorter, Quinn's mom got better. When school let out for Thanksgiving, Quinn and his mom returned to their farm.

When Dad took Mom for a checkup at the hospital next spring, they dropped Quinn off with Papa.

"There's something I want to show you at the pond, Quinn," Papa said, his eyes twinkling.

There, floating among the mallards, were two full-grown American wigeons.

Quinn was sure it was his underdog duckling, who had returned to the place where they had both learned that part of being brave is being who you are.

Questions

1. Why do you think Quinn felt like crying when Papa put his arm around him?

2. How is living in the city different from living on a farm? How is it alike?

3. Why do you think Quinn liked being at the pond?

4. How do you think the duckling came to be at the pond?

5. Why did the kids make fun of Quinn?

6. If you were in Quinn's class, what could you do to make him feel welcome?

7. What does "underdog" mean? Have you ever felt like an underdog?

8. Why was the duckling taken away?

9. Describe a time when you were brave.

10. What kinds of water birds and other wildlife can you see in the pictures? Which birds appear in spring? Summer? Fall? (Answers below.)

11. Count how many ducklings are in each duck family. Which duck family looks most like yours?

12. What water birds live near you?

Water birds and wildlife found in this book: **SPRING**: mallard duck (p.9); **SUMMER**: Canada goose, crayfish, dragonfly, frog, gull, mallard duck, pelican (p.13); American wigeon, mallard duck, sandpiper (p.14); American wigeon (p.17); Canada goose (p.18); **FALL**: Canada goose, gull, mallard duck (p.26); **NEXT SPRING**: American wigeon, gull, mallard duck (p.29).

Sally **Meadows**

Sally Meadows, MSc, BEd, is an award-winning author, recording artist, and speaker from Saskatoon, Saskatchewan. A former scientist, children's entertainer, and educator, Sally loves to share her passion for science and the natural world through her books. This is Sally's fourth book for kids. Her other titles include *The Two Trees* (2015, Your Nickel's Worth Publishing), *Beneath That Star* (2015, Word Alive Press), and *When Sleeping Birds Fly: 365 Amazing Facts About The Animal Kingdom* (2018, Siretona Creative). Connect with Sally online at www.sallymeadows.com, sally@sallymeadows.com, @SallyMeadows, www.instagram.com/sallymeadowsmusic and also at www.facebook.com/SallyMeadowsMusic.

Olha **Tkachenko**

Olha Tkachenko is a Ukrainian-Canadian artist and illustrator from Toronto, Ontario. Olha was born in Ukraine into a family of artists, and started drawing and painting at a young age. After her education, she worked in fine arts, and interior design and decoration. Olha began doing freelance book illustrations in 2008, and has participated in art shows in Ukraine, Canada, and France. She moved with her family to Canada in 2014, where she founded her company, Little Big Me, and happily creates art full time. Connect with Olha online at: www.sonyaolee.net, www.littlebig.me and www.instagram.com/littlebig.me.